RiO

Greetings from Rio!

HarperFestival is an imprint of HarperCollins Publishers.

Rio: Greetings from Rio!
Rio © 2010 Twentieth Century Fox Film Corporation. All rights reserved.
Printed in the United States of America. No part of this book may be used or reproduced in any
manner whatsoever without written permission except in the case of brief quotations embodied in
critical articles and reviews. For information address HarperCollins Children's Books, a division of
HarperCollins Publishers, 10 East 53rd Street, New York, NY 10022.
www.harpercollinschildrens.com
Library of Congress catalog card number: 2010929548
ISBN 978-0-06-202266-0
Typography by Rick Farley
11 12 13 14 15 CWM 10 9 8 7 6 5 4 3 2 1
❖
First Edition

RiO

Greetings from Rio!

Adapted by Benjamin Harper

Based on the motion picture screenplay by Todd R. Jones and Earl Richey Jones

HARPER FESTIVAL

An Imprint of HarperCollins*Publishers*

Greetings from Rio!

I'm Blu—a rare blue Spix's Macaw, which is a kind of parrot. I come from the rain forests of Brazil, but I was taken from my home as a baby. I was raised in Minnesota by my friend Linda. Now I'm back in Rio de Janeiro, a city in Brazil, to save my species!

I'll show you some of the sights here in Rio. I'll also introduce you to my friends, and describe some of the adventures I've had since I've been here. Rio is a very exciting city—I hope you like it as much as I do!

Rio de Janeiro means "January River."
It's one of the biggest cities in South America!
The city's nickname is "the Marvelous City."
From what I saw when I got here, I believed it.
Linda and I saw beaches, lush forests,
and beautiful mountains.

Dr. Tulio Monteiro is the person who brought us here. He studies birds. He's trying to protect us from deforestation and from people who want to capture us! He works at the Conservation Center, where birds like me are kept. Some are sick; some are rare. There's another bird here just like me.

Jewel is the bird I came here to meet. She's a macaw, too. She was kept in a special area of the Conservation Center that looked like her rain forest home. There were streams and lots of trees. But Jewel didn't want to be locked up—she wanted to be free! She wanted me to help her escape!

Sylvio the security guard secretly plays samba music—
the music of Carnavale! When he's not working, he'll wear a
brightly colored costume and practice for the big parade!

Nigel is a cockatoo, another kind of bird. He works for smugglers who sell birds like Jewel and me for a lot of money. He helped kidnap us from the Conservation Center. A boy named Fernando took us to a warehouse where lots of other smuggled birds were being kept—they were planning to take us away on a plane! After Jewel tried to escape, the smugglers chained us together at the ankle.

Jewel and I escaped, but Nigel followed us. As we ran through the streets, everyone in Rio was watching a soccer game—or football as they call it in Brazil—and cheering! Football is a very popular sport in Brazil. We were chased through a crowded neighborhood on the outskirts of the main city.

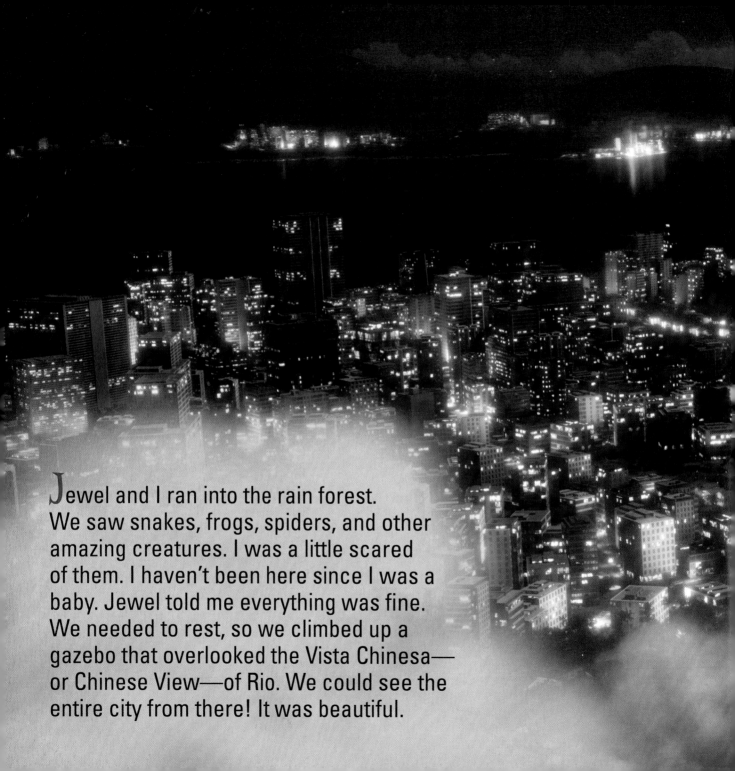

Jewel and I ran into the rain forest. We saw snakes, frogs, spiders, and other amazing creatures. I was a little scared of them. I haven't been here since I was a baby. Jewel told me everything was fine. We needed to rest, so we climbed up a gazebo that overlooked the Vista Chinesa— or Chinese View—of Rio. We could see the entire city from there! It was beautiful.

From the Vista Chinesa, we could see Sugar Loaf Mountain. Sugar Loaf is at the entrance of Guanabara Bay. It's 1,296 feet tall! There's a glass-paneled cable car that runs to the top of the mountain. Sugar Loaf is made of mostly granite and quartz!

Back in the rain forest, Jewel and I met some toucans. Toucans have long, colorful bills! Rafael wanted to help us get the chain off our legs. He said he'd take us to his friend Luiz, who would know just what to do.

Nigel was still looking for us. He thought he'd have better luck with help. He chose monkeys! Marmosets, to be exact. Marmosets live in the tops of trees in the jungle, and they eat bugs and fruit. They like to live in family groups. They also like shiny objects!

Flying lesson! Since I lived in a cage most of my life, I never learned how to fly. Rafael and Jewel wanted to teach me, so we could get around faster. They took me to a ledge overlooking Rio. Hang gliders soared by. I was scared to jump.

But I did! I couldn't fly, and Jewel and I tumbled toward the ground, until we landed on a hang glider's wing. We drifted over the bay. I looked across and saw a giant statue atop a beautiful mountain. Mount Corcovado is one of the biggest attractions in Rio! People come from all over the world to see the statue that overlooks the city. It's so big that it can be seen from miles away!

We landed right on the beach—another of the most popular attractions of Rio. Since Rio is right on the Atlantic Ocean, it is lined with beaches. People love to come and sun themselves on the beautiful white sand!

We decided to take a trolley to find Luiz. But first, we went to a party! Rafael is friends with some birds named Kipo, Nico, and Pedro, who run a club in a fruit stand. Everyone there was having fun! There was singing and dancing, and lots of fruit! I had never tasted fruit before. I loved it!

Jewel and I took a trolley called the Santa Teresa Historic Tram. We were on the roof of the trolley, so we got the best view. Up and up we went in the hills overlooking the city. We could hear everyone getting ready for a big celebration.

We finally met Luiz—we were scared of him at first. He's a bulldog! He removed the chain that was holding us together.

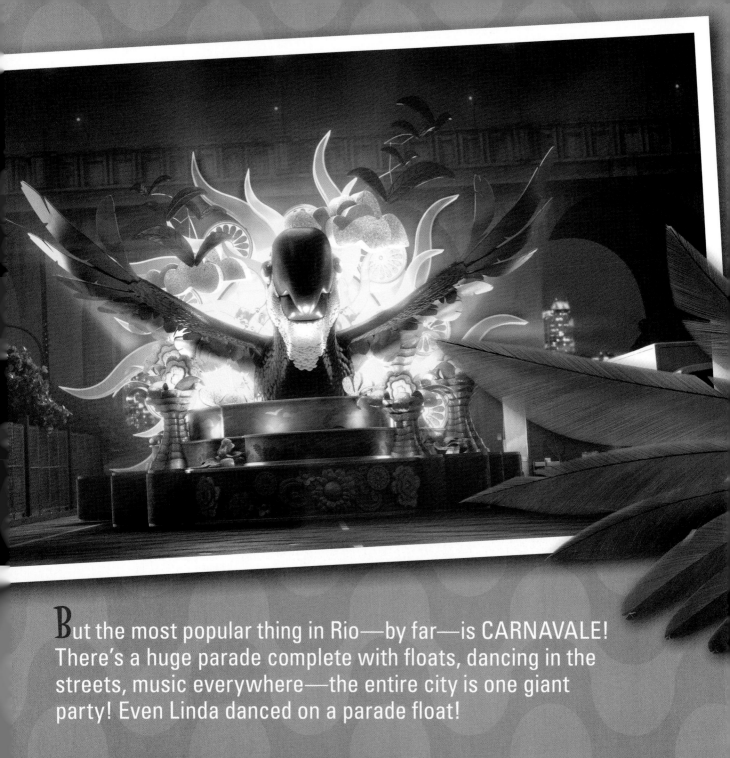

But the most popular thing in Rio—by far—is CARNAVALE! There's a huge parade complete with floats, dancing in the streets, music everywhere—the entire city is one giant party! Even Linda danced on a parade float!

Working together, we're now all safe from the smugglers. I even learned how to fly!

Jewel and I are back in the rain forest, where we belong. All our friends come to visit us. You should come to visit, too!